SUPERHERO GRAN

To the memory of
Lillian and Mary, my
very own Superhero Grans!
With love J.B.

To Superhero Grans
everywhere!
With love T.K.

First published 2020 by Nosy Crow Ltd
The Crow's Nest
14 Baden Place, Crosby Row
London SE1 1YW

ISBN 978 1 78800 546 3 (HB) · ISBN 978 1 78800 547 0 (PB)

www.nosycrow.com

Nosy Crow and associated logos are trademarks and/or registered trademarks of Nosy Crow Ltd.
Text © Timothy Knapman 2020 · Illustrations © Joe Berger 2020

The right of Timothy Knapman to be identified as the author of this work
and of Joe Berger to be identified as the illustrator of this work has been asserted.

Printed in China
Papers used by Nosy Crow are made from wood grown in sustainable forests.

1 3 5 7 9 8 6 4 2 (HB) · 1 3 5 7 9 8 6 4 2 (PB)

SUPERHERO GRAN

TIMOTHY KNAPMAN

illustrated by

JOE BERGER

nosy crow

All grans are great and full of **fun,**
but we know one who can
make **every** day the **very** best . . .

. . . our

SUPERHE

She lives in this **amazing** house that's brilliant to **explore** . . .

where lots of **toys** and **games** to play spill out of every drawer.

She **helps** us dress up in her glasses, scarves and coats and hats.

No one can
recognise us two . . .

we even **fool** her cats!

Then, from her make-up table,

she takes . . .

lipsticks,

powders,

cream,   and . . .

. . . look at us! KA-POW!
We'd make a supervillain scream!

She has this biscuit tin
that's **full** of **every**
kind of **treat.**

Gran's not like Mum
and Dad, who say,
"You've had **enough** to eat!"

She tells us **funny** stories
and they **really** are the **best**.
Our **favourite** is the one about . . .

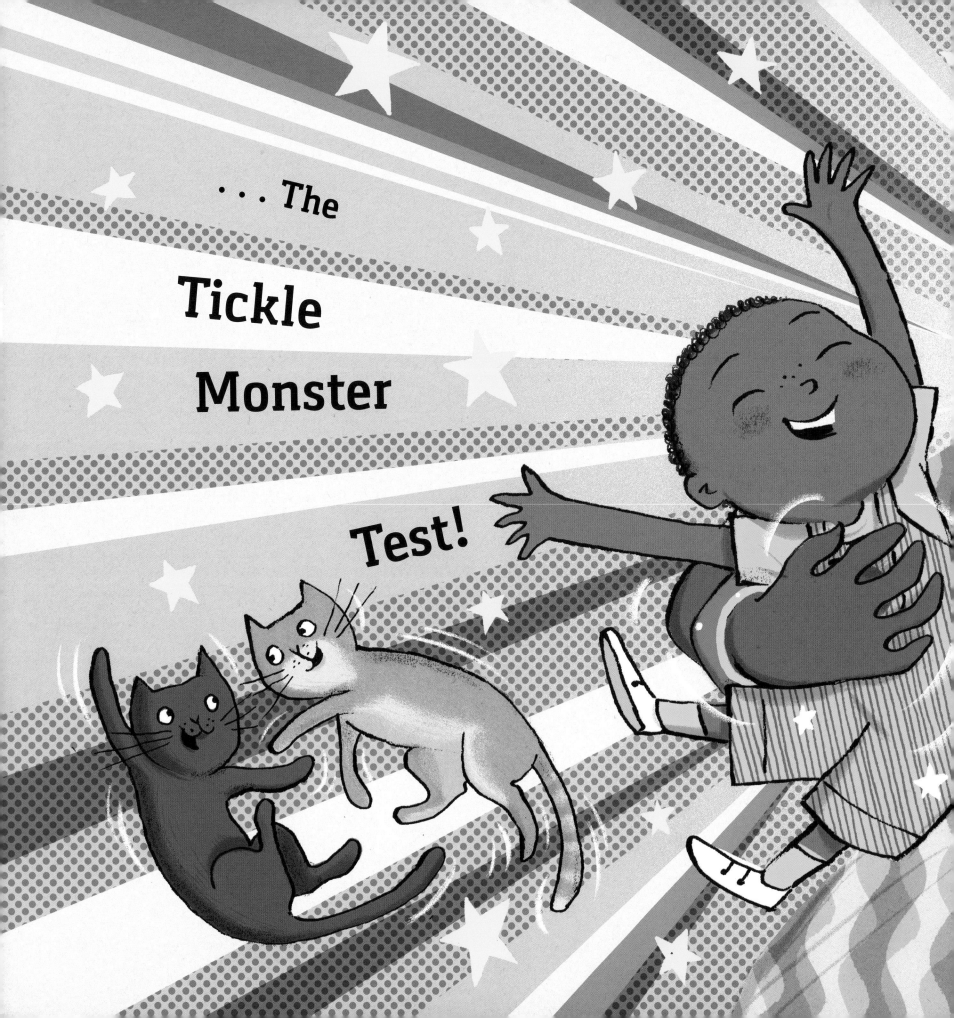

. . . The

Tickle

Monster

Test!

She's very **good** at gardening.

She **loves** her plants and flowers.

They're **great** for playing

hide-and-seek . . .

Gran can't find us for
hours!

We know she can't lift buildings or go **whooshing** through the sky, but she's our **hero** just the same and here's the reason **why** . . .

When it is nearly home time
but we want to stay with **Gran,**
though Mum and Dad
might both say no,
our Gran will have a **plan.**

She'll call up Mum and Dad and say,
"They simply **have** to stay
and have . . .

. . . **a super sleepover**

to end our super day."

"Oh, Gran," we say, "how do you do the **SUPER** things you do?" Gran says, "Because **I love you so . . .**